Dear Parents:

Congratulations! Your child is taking the first steps on an exciting journey. The destination? Independent reading!

STEP INTO READING® will help your child get there. The program offers five steps to reading success. Each step includes fun stories and colorful art or photographs. In addition to original fiction and books with favorite characters, there are Step into Reading Non-Fiction Readers, Phonics Readers and Boxed Sets, Sticker Readers, and Comic Readers—a complete literacy program with something to interest every child.

Learning to Read, Step by Step!

Ready to Read   Preschool–Kindergarten
• big type and easy words • rhyme and rhythm • picture clues
For children who know the alphabet and are eager to begin reading.

Reading with Help   Preschool–Grade 1
• basic vocabulary • short sentences • simple stories
For children who recognize familiar words and sound out new words with help.

Reading on Your Own   Grades 1–3
• engaging characters • easy-to-follow plots • popular topics
For children who are ready to read on their own.

Reading Paragraphs   Grades 2–3
• challenging vocabulary • short paragraphs • exciting stories
For newly independent readers who read simple sentences with confidence.

Ready for Chapters   Grades 2–4
• chapters • longer paragraphs • full-color art
For children who want to take the plunge into chapter books but still like colorful pictures.

STEP INTO READING® is designed to give every child a successful reading experience. The grade levels are only guides; children will progress through the steps at their own speed, developing confidence in their reading. The F&P Text Level on the back cover serves as another tool to help you choose the right book for your child.

Remember, a lifetime love of reading starts with a single step!

W9-BYT-311

Visit us on the Web!
StepIntoReading.com
randomhousekids.com

Educators and librarians, for a variety of teaching tools, visit us at RHTeachersLibrarians.com

Library of Congress Cataloging-in-Publication Data
Briggs, Raymond, author, illustrator.
The snowman and the snowdog / Raymond Briggs.
pages cm. — (Step into reading. Step 1)
"Adapted from the book The Snowman and the Snowdog, first published in Great Britain by Penguin Books, London, in 2012, and subsequently by Random House Children's Books, New York, in 2014."
Summary: Billy makes a snowman and a snowdog that come to life and take him on a magical adventure at the North Pole.
ISBN 978-0-385-38734-7 (trade pbk.) — ISBN 978-0-385-38735-4 (lib. bdg.) —
ISBN 978-0-385-38736-1 (ebook)
[1. Snowmen—Fiction. 2. Dogs—Fiction. 3. Santa Claus—Fiction. 4. North Pole—Fiction.]
I. Title.
PZ7.B7646Snn 2015 [E]—dc23 2014025972

Printed in the United States of America
10 9 8 7 6 5 4 3 2 1

This book has been officially leveled by using the F&P Text Level Gradient™ Leveling System.

The Snowman™
AND THE SNOWDOG

based on characters created by
Raymond Briggs
adapted by Anna Membrino
illustrated by Maggie Downer

Random House 🏠 New York

This is Billy.

Billy makes a snowman.

He makes a snowdog, too!

Look!

The Snowman and
the Snowdog
have come to life!

The Snowman takes
Billy's hand.

Billy holds the
Snowdog.

Now they are flying!

11

They fly high.
They fly far!

But where are they going?

To the North Pole!

There are many
snowpeople at
the North Pole.

The snowmen line up.
Billy and the Snowdog
line up, too.

It is a race!

Ready, set, GO!

The snowmen go fast.

Billy and the Snowdog
go faster!

Oh, no!

Here comes a penguin!

The Snowdog sticks
his nose over
the finish line.

Billy and the Snowdog
win the race!

Santa Claus is at the
finish line.

He gives Billy a present.

It is time to fly home.

Billy opens

his present.

It is a magical
dog collar!

Now the Snowdog is a real dog!